Happy hopping to my two favorite librarians, Janine and Ann,
and also to my toad-ally awesome friend Peggy. HOP-TO-IT!!
—P. S.

For Tim
—J. M.

Carolrhoda Books, Inc.
A division of Lerner Publishing Group
241 First Avenue North
Minneapolis, MN 55401 U.S.A.

Website address: www.carolrhodabooks.com

Library of Congress Cataloging-in-Publication Data

Schnetzler, Pattie L., 1952–
    Fast 'n' Snappy / by Pattie Schnetzler ; illustrated by Jane Manning.
       p.   cm.
    Summary: Fast the alligator and Snappy the frog, the best pardner a Hop-to-It Express rider
ever had, speed west with an important letter from President A. Blinkin while Gila Joe and his
snakes try to stop them at every turn. Includes facts about the Pony Express.
    ISBN: 1–57505–539–2 (lib. bdg. : alk. paper)
    [1. Postal service—History—Fiction. 2. Alligators—Fiction. 3. Frogs—Fiction. 4. Robbers and
outlaws—Fiction. 5. West (U.S.)—History—Fiction. 6. Humorous stories. 7. Pony express.]
    I. Manning, Jane K., ill. II. Title.
PZ7.S36433Fas 2004
[E]—dc21
                                                                                2003006413

Manufactured in the United States of America
1 2 3 4 5 6 – DP – 09 08 07 06 05 04

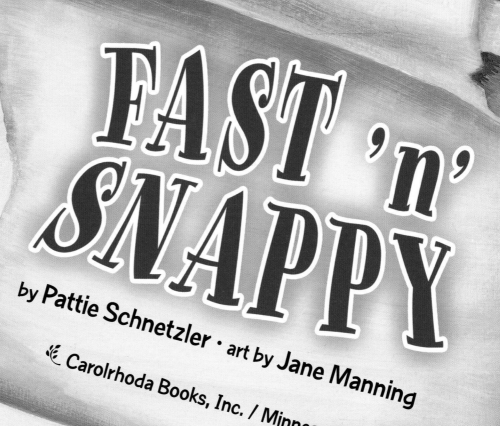

FAST 'n' SNAPPY

by Pattie Schnetzler • art by Jane Manning

Carolrhoda Books, Inc. / Minneapolis

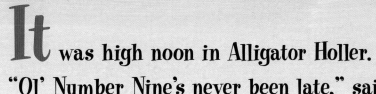

It was high noon in Alligator Holler.

"Ol' Number Nine's never been late," said Hoppity Cassidy to the other Hop-to-It Express riders. "And today, she's bringing an URGENT letter from the president. A letter we have to rush west."

"Don't worry, boys," said Fast. "Me and Snappy are hopping the first part of the relay. We'll make up the lost time. But it'll be up to the next rider to hop it on from there."

"I'm not worried about you and Snappy," said Hoppity Cassidy. "I'm worried about Gila Joe. Remember when he was a Hop-to-It Express rider? He was loyal until he saw that his face wasn't on the first Express stamp."

"Then," added Slim, "steam came outta his ears when he wasn't picked to make the first historical hop."

"After that," said Hoppity, "Joe started stealin' mail and rustlin' Hop-to-It frogs and horned toads."

Fast nodded. "But even worse, he betrayed *The Oath.*"

THROUGH RAIN 'N' SNOW 'N' SLEET,
ACROSS THE DESERT HEAT,
WE'LL HOP DOWN ANY TRAIL
TO BRING THE U.S. MAIL.

Just then a whistle shrieked, and the train screeched to a halt. President A. Blinkin stepped onto the platform.

"Sorry we're late," he began. "We were held up by Gila Joe and his gang. They were looking for this." He removed a letter from his stovepipe hat. "But I gave them Mrs. Blinkin's grocery list, instead. This letter welcomes our newest state, Cactus Gulch, into our great Union. I've brought it as far as the train goes, and now I'm trusting it to you."

Fast took the letter and hid it under Snappy's saddle. "The Hop-to-It Express will deliver your letter to Cactus Gulch. Snappy and I made our oath, and by gumbo, we're stickin' to it."

Fast tipped his coonskin cap, put heels to Snappy, and . . .

HOP-TO-IT! They were off!

The sun stood high when Fast 'n' Snappy approached the Road Runner Sink Station.

"GREAT SWAMPS!" roared Fast, as he spied Lickety Split, the stationmaster, hangin' by his spurs. "What happened?"

"When Gila Joe discovered that President Blinkin tricked 'im, he vowed to stop Blinkin's urgent letter," said Lickety. "He kidnapped yer relief rider and rustled all my horned toads."

"Nothin's gonna stop the Hop-to-It from gettin' to Cactus Gulch," said Fast. "Me and Snappy'll hop this letter to the next station ourselves. We made our oath, and by gumbo, we're stickin' to it."

Fast tipped his coonskin cap, put heels to Snappy, and . . .

The sun was sliding into the western mountains when Fast 'n' Snappy stopped at Sidewinder Station.

It was so quiet, you could've heard a letter floating on the wind.

"Somethin' is wrong," whispered Fast. "The next rider should be here waitin' fer us."

Snappy darted his tongue, tasting the air for trouble. Something didn't look right. The fence posts were swaying. And the barbs on the fence looked like fangs.

"SNAKES!" roared Fast, but it was too late. They were surrounded.

"Well, well, well," said Gila Joe. "Look who's reached the end of the mail trail."

"Oh no, we haven't," whispered Fast to Snappy. "Get ready."

Snappy dug in his froggy toes, and then . . .

he exploded into motion. Them snake varmints followed close on his heels. Right over left and under. Left over right and under. Snappy zipped round and round 'til Joe and his gang were knotted up purty as a package.

"I'd invite ya along," said Fast. "But it appears yer all tied up!"

He tipped his coonskin cap, put heels to Snappy, and

HOP-TO-IT! They were off!

Fast peered into the growing darkness. "Looks like it's up to us to get President Blinkin's letter to Cactus Gulch."

Snappy croaked softly. He was so tuckered out, he barely had any hop left in him.

Fast sized up the situation. "There's a spot just ahead, right below Wild Water Dam. We'll stop there and catch a few winks."

Both were asleep before their heads hit the sand of the dry riverbed.

Hours later, Fast 'n' Snappy awoke to rumbling. The noise quickly became a roar. Fast looked up and gawked. Gila Joe stood atop the dam waving a fistful of sticks. He had taken Wild Water Dam apart while they slept!

"RISE AND SHINE!" shouted Joe.

A wall of water roared toward them, churning and foaming like a mad dog.

"DIG IN YER FROGGY TOES!" yelled Fast. But the flood swept Fast 'n' Snappy under. Down they plunged, twisting and turning and choking.

Fast had almost given up when the runaway river spit him out. Jumping to his feet, Fast searched for his frog.

"SNAPPY!" he hollered. But no hoppy croak answered.

Fast's heart ached. Snappy was gone, along with President Blinkin's letter.

After searching all morning for Snappy, Fast found a scattering of toad tracks.

"Lickety Split's toads musta got away after they were stolen from the Road Runner Sink Station!" exclaimed Fast. "It looks like they're headed for the next station."

Fast followed the tracks that led, sure enough, to the No Return Station. "Well, well, well." A cold voice sent chills up Fast's spine. "Hope you enjoyed your swim," said Gila Joe. "Now hand it over."

"I lost Blinkin's letter in yer little flood," answered Fast.

Joe whistled. His snakes, Sss-spit and Sss-spike, picked up Fast and shook him 'til his teeth chattered.

"NO LETTER?" bellowed Joe. "TIE 'IM UP!"

Fast hung his head. He'd let down Snappy. He'd let down President Blinkin. But worst of all, he'd let down the Hop-to-It Express.

The moon was rising when a thunderous croak rose from the valley. A green streak sped toward Fast. It was Snappy! He sped so fast that he knocked down Sss-spit and Sss-spike like two bowling pins!

"SSSS-STRIKE, PARDNER!" yelled Fast.

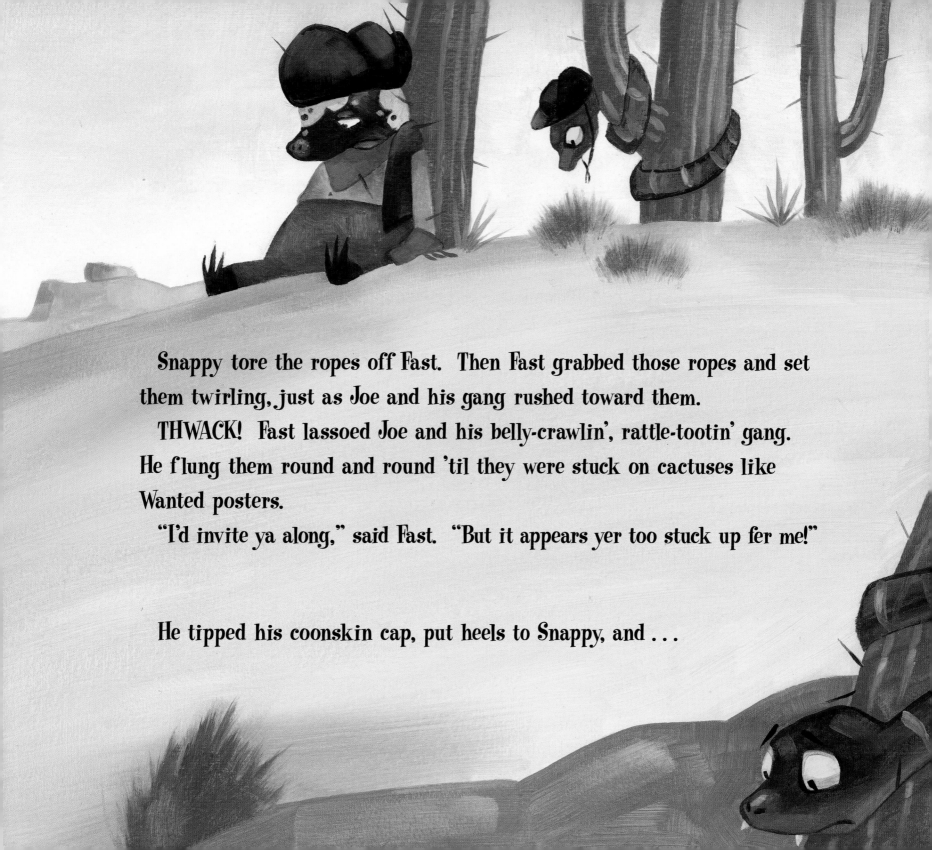

Snappy tore the ropes off Fast. Then Fast grabbed those ropes and set
them twirling, just as Joe and his gang rushed toward them.

THWACK! Fast lassoed Joe and his belly-crawlin', rattle-tootin' gang.
He flung them round and round 'til they were stuck on cactuses like
Wanted posters.

"I'd invite ya along," said Fast. "But it appears yer too stuck up fer me!"

He tipped his coonskin cap, put heels to Snappy, and . . .

HOP-TO-IT! They were off! Fast reached under the saddle and checked for the letter. It was still there! His heart swelled bigger 'n a giant catfish. "Yer the best pardner a Hop-to-It rider could have."

Snappy glurped hoppily.

Just when they thought they could hop no more, Fast 'n' Snappy reached Echo Canyon. Fast glanced over his shoulder and saw Gila Joe and his gang racing toward them.

"This is it," Fast panted.

Snappy croaked a faint reply. A faint croak echoed back. Suddenly, Fast had a whopper of an idea. "Let's make ourselves a cavalry!" he whispered to Snappy.

"BANG, BANG. THE CAVALRY'S COMIN'," yelled Fast.
"BANG, BANG. THE CAVALRY'S COMIN'," the canyon walls yelled back.

"WHOOP, WHOOP, WAHOO," yelled Fast.
"WHOOP, WHOOP, WAHOO," answered the canyon walls.

As soon as they heard Gila Joe yell, "The cavalry's comin'!" Snappy
hopped back and forth kicking up dirt and sand until it looked like a
tornado. The west wind blew that dust tornado smack into Gila Joe and
his gang.

Just then, Fast 'n' Snappy heard a bugle blare.
IT WAS THE REAL CAVALRY!

"Heard you might be in trouble," the colonel yelled as he raced toward them.

Fast grinned and pointed toward the canyon. "Looks to me like they're the ones in trouble!"

The cavalry took off after Gila Joe and his gang.

On the other side of Echo Canyon, Fast spied Cactus Gulch. They'd made it!

CACTUS GULCH

Fast handed the urgent letter to the mayor.

The mayor cleared his throat, "This letter's from President A. Blinkin." The townsfolk grew quiet as they lent an ear.

ON THIS DAY,
HONOR AND GLORY AND PRIDE
ARE WHAT WE FEEL INSIDE
AS WE CELEBRATE THE DAY
YOU JOINED THE U.S.A.
CACTUS GULCH, WELCOME TO THE UNION!
—President A. Blinkin

The crowd cheered as the wind took to whistlin' *America the Beautiful.* The clouds waved and flapped like the flag, Old Glory.

Fast removed his cap. "Pardner," he said to Snappy. "We made our oath, and by gumbo, we stuck to it!"

A Fast 'n' Snappy History of the Pony Express

In 1860, there were no telephones, televisions, or radios to bring news. There were no airplanes, and trains had not yet traveled farther west than the Missouri River. Mail from east to west took about 25 days to deliver by stagecoach and 22 days by boat. People who lived in the west were eager to hear news—the faster the better.

On January 27, 1860, a businessman named William Russell had an idea that would shorten mail delivery time to 10 days. His idea was to use horses and riders to run a gigantic relay race to deliver the eastern mail to California. The proposed route was about 2,000 miles from the eastern end in St. Joseph, Missouri, to the western end in Sacramento, California.

Russell went to work. He had station houses built every 10 to 15 miles along the route—almost 190 in all! He bought 500 of the toughest, fastest horses around. And he hired brave, young boys to ride.

Each rider had to take an oath before he was hired. In this oath, he promised not to use bad language, not to drink alcohol or gamble, and not

to be mean to the animals. He also promised to be a gentleman. The riders adopted the motto, "The mail must go through."

The first run of the Pony Express was on April 3, 1860—just 65 days after the initial idea! Pony Express riders changed horses at each station. Each rider rode about 75 miles, riding 6 to 8 different horses, before turning the mail over to a new rider, who would complete his piece of the relay.

The fastest ride on record was in March of 1861, when the Pony Express sped President Abraham Lincoln's inaugural address from St. Joseph, Missouri, to California. It was safely delivered in just 7 days and 17 hours.

Although a great part of American history, the Pony Express didn't last long. Just 18 months after it started, the telegraph, a new invention by Samuel Morse, made communication even faster. By 1862, wires for the telegraph spanned the Sierra Nevada Mountains, connecting east and west. The telegraph took just minutes to accomplish what the Pony Express had done in days.

Echo Canyon

No Return Station

Cactus Gulch

Wild Water Dam